panda series

PANDA books are for first readers beginning to make their own way through books.

D0550732

ANOTHER GREAT DANNY STORY

Collect all the **Danny** stories
in the PANDA SERIES

Pageboy Danny

BRIANÓG BRADY DAWSON

• Pictures by Michael Connor •

THE O'BRIEN PRESS
DUBLIN

First published 2006 by The O'Brien Press Ltd,
20 Victoria Road, Dublin 6, Ireland.
Tel: +353 1 4923333; Fax: +353 1 4922777
E-mail: books@obrien.ie
Website: www.obrien.ie

ISBN 10: 0-86278-950-8

ISBN 13: 978-0-86278-950-3

British Library Cataloguing-in-Publication Data
Dawson, Brianog Brady
Pageboy Danny. - (Panda books ; 34)
1.Brown, Danny (Fictitious character) - Juvenile fiction
2.Children's stories
I.Title II.Connor, Michael
823.9'14[J]

The O'Brien Press receives assistance from

1 2 3 4 5 6 7 8 9 10
06 07 08 09 10

Typesetting, layout, editing, design: The O'Brien Press Ltd
Printing: Cox & Wyman Ltd

For Adam, with love

Can YOU spot the panda hidden in the story?

Danny Brown was playing
with his dog, Keeno.
He was teaching him
how to do tricks.

'**Sit**!' cried Danny.

Keeno sat up straight.

'Look, Mum!' cried Danny.
'Keeno can do a **trick**.'

But Mum wasn't listening.
She was feeding
Danny's little sister, Susie.

Danny took a sausage
from Susie's dish.
He held it in front of Keeno.

'**Beg**,' cried Danny.
Keeno stood on his back legs.
He held out his paws.

'Look, Granny!' cried Danny.
'Keeno has learned
another trick.'

But Granny wasn't listening.
She was trying on
her new hat.

Danny pushed Keeno down.
'**Play dead**,' he cried.
Keeno lay on his side
and put his head
on the floor.

Danny rubbed Keeno's tummy.
'Roll over,' he said.
Keeno rolled over
and put his four legs
in the air.

'Look, Grandpa!' said Danny.
'Keeno can do lots of tricks.'

Grandpa put down
his newspaper.
He looked at Keeno.

He saw Keeno **sit**.

He saw Keeno **beg**.

He saw Keeno **play dead**.

He saw Keeno **roll over**.

'Can Keeno **fetch**?'
asked Grandpa.

Granny's new hat
was on the table.
'Watch this!' cried Danny.
He threw the hat in the air.
'**Fetch**, Keeno,' he yelled.

Keeno jumped.

He caught the hat.

Grandpa was amazed.

'Keeno is a very clever dog,
Danny,' he said.

Grandpa rubbed Keeno's
shiny coat.

Then he had an idea.
'Keeno looks great,' he said.
'And he does what he's told.
Let's take him to the Dog Show
on Saturday, Danny.'

'**COOL**!'
shouted Danny.

He put on Granny's hat.
He danced for joy.
'We're going to the Dog Show!'
he sang.

Just then Granny appeared.
'**My new hat**!' she cried.
'That's my new hat
for Saturday!'

She snatched her hat
from Danny.

'Are you going to the Dog Show
too, Granny?' asked Danny.

Mum laughed.
'Don't be silly, Danny,'
she said. 'Uncle Ted's wedding
is on Saturday. We're all going.'

'Oh no!' cried Danny. '**I** can't.
'I'm going to the Dog Show
with Grandpa.'
Then he had an idea.
'**You** go to the wedding,'
he said. '**I'll** take Keeno
to the Dog Show.'

'No, Danny,' said Mum.
'You **have** to go
to the wedding.
You're the **pageboy**.'
'What's a pageboy?'
asked Danny crossly.

'You'll be in charge
of the wedding rings,'
explained Mum.

Danny wasn't happy.
He folded his arms.
He stared at Mum.

'I don't know how
to be a pageboy!' he said.

'Don't worry, Danny,'
said Mum.
'I'll tell you what to do.
And you'll wear special clothes.
You'll look great!'

'It sounds just like
the Dog Show!'
chuckled Grandpa.

Suddenly Danny had
a wonderful idea.
He knelt beside Keeno.
He hugged him.

'You can do your tricks
at the wedding, Keeno!'
he whispered.
'It will be just like
the Dog Show!'

On Saturday morning,
the house was very noisy.
Everyone was busy.

Granny was running upstairs
and downstairs.
'I can't find my new hat,'
she squealed.

'I put it in the boot of the car,'
sighed Grandpa.
'It will be safe there.'

Susie was screaming.
She had spilt her milk
on her new dress.

'Oh no, Susie!' cried Mum.
'Now I have to clean you up
again!'

'Keeno has to be cleaned up
for the wedding too,'
said Danny.
Mum stared at Danny.

'Are you mad?' she cried.
'Keeno is **not** going
to the wedding!'

Danny was shocked.
He looked at Keeno's sad face.
'Don't worry, Keeno,'
he whispered.
'I have a plan!'

Then he sneaked upstairs
with Keeno.

Danny took Keeno
into the bathroom.
He scrubbed him clean.
Then he got Keeno's
new, red doggie coat.

'Woof!' barked Keeno.
He started to run downstairs.

Danny ran after him.
'Keeno!' he said.
'Today is an important day.
You have to wear
special clothes!'

Danny put the doggie coat
on Keeno.

Then he sneaked out
to the car with Keeno.
He opened the boot.
'Jump in, Keeno,'
he said quietly.

Danny closed the boot
and ran back to the house.

Mum was upstairs.
'Danny!' she yelled.
'It's time to get dressed
for the wedding. Hurry.'

Mum gave Danny
a white shirt.
It had frills
all down the front.

Then she gave him
a blue bow tie.

Danny made a face.
'Yuck!' he said.

Then Mum gave Danny
a pair of white stockings.
'These will look nice with
the knickerbockers,' she said.

'**Knicker–what**?'
screamed Danny.
'Those clothes are **stupid**!
I'm not wearing them.'

Danny ran downstairs.

Mum ran after him.
'Danny!' she said crossly.
'Today is an important day.
You have to wear
special clothes.'

Danny hid in the garden.
Mum looked everywhere.
'**Danny**!' she yelled.

Granny looked everywhere.
'**Danny**!' she squealed.
They couldn't find him.

Grandpa saw Danny
hiding in the shed.

'Danny,' he said.
'I have a big surprise for you.
But first, you have to
do your job at the wedding.'

Danny peeped out of the shed.
'What's the surprise?' he asked.

'I'm going to take you and
Keeno to the Dog Show!'
promised Grandpa.
'We'll go after the wedding.'

'Yippee!' cried Danny.
He hugged Grandpa.
He raced upstairs.

He put on the frilly
shirt and the bow tie.

He put on the
silly stockings.

He even put on the
knickerbockers.

In the car, Mum gave Danny
a little velvet box.
'The rings are in that,' she said.
'Mind them carefully.
I'll tell you what to do
when we're in the church.'

Soon they reached the church.
There were ribbons
and flowers everywhere.
'Oh dear!' said Granny.
'I forgot my hat!'

'I'll go to the car and get it,'
whispered Grandpa.

Grandpa got Granny's hat.

The ribbons were torn.

The flowers were chewed.

'My hat is a **mess**!'

said Granny.

'Keeno was hiding in the boot!'

said Grandpa.

'**And he's escaped**!'

Oh no, thought Danny.

I think it's time for **me** to hide!

He slid under his seat.

Mum nudged Danny.

'Bring the rings up now,'

she said in a low voice.

Danny took the two rings
out of the box.

He began to walk slowly
up to the top of the church.

Everyone was quiet.

Everyone was watching Danny.

Nobody saw what was coming
in the church door.

Keeno came into the church.
He saw Danny.

'Woof!' he barked happily.
**'Woof! Woof!
Woof!'**

Keeno jumped on Danny.
One of the rings flew out of
Danny's hand.
'**Fetch**, Keeno, **fetch**!'
cried Danny.

Keeno soared into the air.

He opened his mouth.

He caught one of the rings.

Danny clapped.

'Well done, Keeno!' he cheered.

Danny looked at Grandpa.
'What do you think of that?'
he shouted.
Grandpa's mouth was
wide open.

Danny looked
around the church.
Everyone's mouth
was wide open.

'They all want to fetch!'
laughed Danny.
'Let's show them
some more tricks, Keeno!'

Danny held the other ring
over Keeno's head.
'**Beg**, Keeno,' he ordered.

But Keeno lay still.
He didn't stand
on his hind legs.
He didn't lift his front paws.

He lay down on the floor
of the church.
He didn't move.

'Look, everyone,' cried Danny.
'Keeno can **play dead**!'

'**Roll over**, Keeno,'
cried Danny.
Keeno didn't move.
Danny began to get worried.

'What's wrong, Keeno?'
he whispered.

Suddenly Keeno coughed.
He coughed and coughed
and coughed and coughed.

'Oh no!' yelled Danny.
'It's the ring!
Keeno has **swallowed**
the ring!'

Mum, Granny and Grandpa
dashed out of their seats.
Mum glared at Danny.
'**Sit**!' she hissed.
'What about Keeno?'
shouted Danny.

Grandpa lifted Keeno
in his arms.
'We'll have to take him
to the vet,' he said.

Danny was shocked.
'But what about
the Dog Show?' he cried.
'Everyone must see
Keeno's tricks.'

'We've seen enough
of Keeno's tricks, Danny,'
said Grandpa.

'We've seen enough
of **your** tricks, too, Danny!'
added Granny.

Mum was furious.
'The vet will deal with Keeno,'
she said. 'And **I'll** deal
with **you**, Danny!'

Danny flopped to the floor.

He lay on his side.

He threw back his head.

He decided to **play dead**.

'I'll never do anything
like this again,' he muttered.
'Never. Never. Never.'

But I think he will, don't you?
Danny's just that kind of kid!